For Ann, who makes every Christmas special ~ S. S.

For my pal, Mary ~ A. E.

Copyright © 2012 by Good Books, Intercourse, PA 17534
International Standard Book Number: 978-1-56148-767-7
Library of Congress Catalog Card Number: 2012000183

Text copyright © Steve Smallman 2012
Illustrations copyright © Alison Edgson 2012
Original edition published in English by Little Tiger Press,
London, England, 2012
LTP/1800/0385/0312 • Printed in China
Library of Congress Cataloging-in-Publication Data
Smallman, Steve.
Puppy's first Christmas / Steve Smallman ; Alison Edgson.
p. cm.
Summary: A new puppy is worried about his family when
the children begin behaving very well and socks are nailed
to the wall, until Cat explains about Christmas time.
ISBN 978-1-56148-767-7 (hardcover : alk. paper) [1. Stories in rhyme.
2. Dogs--Fiction. 3. Animals--Infancy--Fiction. 4. Cats--Fiction.
5. Christmas--Fiction.] I. Edgson, Alison, ill. II. Title.
PZ8.3.S6358Pup 2012
[E]--dc23
2012000183

Puppy's First Christmas

Steve Smallman

Alison Edgson

Good Books

Intercourse, PA 17534, 800/762-7171, www.GoodBooks.com

"What's going on?" cried Puppy
as he skidded on the floor,
Tangled in the tinsel that was
wrapped around his paw.

Everything seemed different,
all sparkly, strange, and new.
"I'd better find the cat!" he panted.
"She'll know what to do!"

"Wake up, Cat!" he cried. "WAKE UP!
How can you be so lazy?
This is an emergency—
THE CHILDREN HAVE GONE CRAZY!
They haven't argued once, and
I've been watching them all day.
And when Mom said, 'It's time for bed,'
they shouted out 'Hooray!'"

"Something weird is happening—it started with that tree. At first I thought they'd brought it in especially for me.

"They covered it
with lights and balls
and chocolates—
what a waste!

"Then told me I was
naughty when I tried
to have a taste!"

"It happens every year," said Cat.
"It's Christmas-time, you see—
A mad, enormous party
that's for all the family!

"Mom goes really bonkers doing
loads and loads of cooking.
They'll never eat it all so we can
'help' when they're not looking!"

"But Cat," the puppy cried,
"they've nailed their socks up
on the wall!
I really just don't understand
this Christmas thing at all!"

"Don't worry, little Pup," said Cat,
"this Christmas thing is fun.
And later, Santa Claus will come
with gifts for everyone!"

"WHO'S SANTA CLAUS?" asked Puppy.
"He's a great old guy!" said Cat.
"He's jolly, plump, and whiskery
and wears a furry hat.

"He'll bring us all a present
while we're fast asleep in bed!"

"Oh, Cat, let's try to stay awake
and meet him!" Puppy said.

They looked out of the window
at the stars so clear and bright
And listened hard for noises on
that crystal Christmas night—
The jingle of a harness and
the stomping of a hoof,
A muffled, jolly "Ho, ho, ho!"
from somewhere on the roof.

"Where's Santa Claus?"
yawned Puppy.
"How much longer
will he take?"

As they waited and they
waited, trying hard
to stay awake.

Cat saw Puppy's eyelids
close, then heard his
gentle snores,

And just as Cat dropped off to sleep,
in came . . .

. . . SANTA CLAUS!

"Wake up, Pup, it's Christmas day!"
said Cat. "Quick, come and see!
Santa left these presents here
for all the family!"
"I've got one, too!" cried Puppy.
"Oh, wow, how cool is that?
Thank you, Santa Claus!"
he woofed and . . .

. . . "Merry Christmas, Cat!"